DO YOU MIND IF I SIT HERE?

Also by James Long and Marcus Youssef

*Winners and Losers**

Also by Marcus Youssef

*Adrift**

*Adventures of Ali & Ali and the aXes of Evil:
A Divertimento for Warlords**

*Ali and Ali: The Deportation Hearings**

*The In-Between**

*Jabber**

*King Arthur's Night and Peter Panties: A Collaboration across
Perceptions of Cognitive Difference** (with Niall McNeil)

*Published by Talonbooks

DO YOU MIND IF I SIT HERE?

a play

James Long
and
Marcus Youssef

foreword by Jiv Parasram

Talonbooks

Talonbooks
9259 Shaughnessy Street, Vancouver, British Columbia, Canada v6p 6r4
talonbooks.com

Talonbooks is located on xʷməθkʷəy̓əm, Sḵwx̱wú7mesh, and səlilwətaɬ Lands.

First printing: 2024
Typeset in Arno
Printed and bound in Canada on 100% post-consumer recycled paper

Cover design by Ginger Sedlarova
Cover photograph by Emily Cooper

Talonbooks acknowledges the financial support of the Canada Council for the Arts, the Government of Canada through the Canada Book Fund, and the Province of British Columbia through the British Columbia Arts Council and the Book Publishing Tax Credit.

Library and Archives Canada Cataloguing in Publication

Title: Do you mind if I sit here? : a play / James Long and Marcus Youssef ; foreword by Jivesh Parasram.
Names: Long, James, 1973- author. | Youssef, Marcus, author. | Parasram, Jivesh, writer of foreword.
Identifiers: Canadiana 20230556337 | ISBN 9781772014495 (softcover)
Subjects: LCGFT: Drama.
Classification: LCC PS8623.O535 D62 2024 | DDC C812/.6—dc23

To Edward Pedersen, caretaker of the
Russian Hall from 2006 to 2016

WRITERS' NOTE

Do you mind if it I sit here? began inside a moment of procrastination in about 2010 as we tried to distract ourselves from the development of another work, *Winners and Losers* (Talonbooks, 2015). Tired of competing inside the often-cruel structure we had devised for that project, we found ourselves rather impolitely rooting around an unlocked closet next door to Theatre Replacement's studio in Vancouver's Russian Hall, where we quickly discovered dozens of cans of 16 mm films. Films that, once we found a working projector (it was a nice long procrastination), appeared to have been produced in the USSR during the mid-part of the twentieth century, and then shipped to Canada through to the mid-1980s in an apparent attempt to lure a scattered Russian diaspora home to the Soviet Union.

The approximately twenty hours worth of disintegrating celluloid included beautifully shot depictions of Soviet successes in the fields of medicine, agriculture, mining, space travel, etc.; a short documentary on an Indigenous population that had the occasional look and flavour of Robert J. Flaherty's 1922 *Nanook of the North*; as well as a pretty bougie little piece called *Moscow at Night* that had an unseen, silent filmmaker cruising the bars, boutiques, and streets of that city. After trying and failing to insert the films into *Winners and Losers*, we returned them to their closet until 2019, when funding from the National Arts Centre's National Creation Fund allowed us to bring a team together and begin exploring how, or even if, these films could somehow become central to a live performance – ideally one that honoured the building we found them in. It was right about then that the world really started shifting under our feet.

Our first full workshop with actors for what would become *Do you mind if I sit here?* took place under mask, distance, and hand-sanitizer protocols in the summer of 2020, four months into the COVID-19 pandemic. Our second period of work coincided with what turned out to be the deadliest weather event in Canadian history, a heat dome that rocked western Canada, killed at least 685 people, and saw the entire town of Lytton, BC, burn in a few hours. The final rehearsal period aligned with the rain and landslides of an atmospheric river that collapsed southern BC's transportation infrastructure, leaving Vancouver cut off from the rest of Canada for five days. These events, which on their own would have reshaped how we make work and think about this place we call home, created in combination a state of constant questioning about how and why we inhabit this world.

It feels important, particularly in light of what landed on the page, to also acknowledge the effect of a less acute though equally impactful conversation that was happening at the time about Canada's Medical Assistance in Dying (MAID) program and the potential to extend it to those living with mental, not just physical, suffering. It is a debate that inserted itself into this work of speculative fiction, which saw a building – once a central gathering spot for generations of families – as being as susceptible to abject loneliness as the inhabitant of the same building that emerges in our work. Yes, as we suggest in the text, buildings can be lonely too.

With all this in tow, it was not surprising that somewhere in the process of imagining, building, and writing, a negotiation with the narrative form and how we tell our stories past, present, and future became central to the project. As well as an associated curiosity specific to the limits of language in trying to shape moments we can no longer understand.

The process of making *Do you mind if I sit here?*, like any new work we develop, is always deeply collaborative. (By the way, for an in-process film of the work, check out vimeo.com/869645072. A trailer for the play can also be found at vimeo.com/869642757.) It starts with us and our multiple procrastinations but soon invites in as vast a collection of disciplines, approaches, and opinions as budgets allow to both trouble and elevate the process. So, while reading, know that the inspiration for these words comes from all those who were kind enough to explore this building that is the Russian Hall with us during this remarkable time – a time that increasingly feels like a future of a future we could have never imagined.

Thanks for reading.

—Jamie and Marcus

FOREWORD
Look Forward, Look Back, Look Away

I'm writing to you from the basement of the Russian Hall, in Strathcona, East Vancouver. Above me is the main hall of the aforementioned, where *Do you mind if I sit here?* was performed. Somewhere in this building – upstairs, I believe, quite a bit upstairs – is the storage room where the old film reels that inspired this project were found. Well, perhaps not "found" so much as stored and then forgotten until they were stumbled upon. I mention this – where I am right now – not just for the sake of novelty, but because place is important.

Do you mind if I sit here? was one of the first indoor pieces of theatre I saw after the COVID-19 pandemic shut down that part of the sector for a while. As such, it was in many ways a surreal experience. I'd seen a fair amount of work at the Russian Hall over the years, but lately my only relationship with the building had been to walk by it. Now I was inside. With other people. Maintaining a safe distance, for them and myself – lest we infect each other with communicable disease through this form of communion. Certainly, the play's title resonated in a distinct way. I remember emailing some praise to Marcus and Jamie – something like, "I really dug the show! ... I *think* I got it?" I have distinct memories of the show, don't get me wrong, but when I think back to those days in general, things get blurry. *Do you mind if I sit here?* is also not what I would call a "naturalistic" piece, by any stretch. Its form felt to me somewhat surreal, somewhat existentialist, perhaps even futurist, but mostly reflective and meditative. The type of reflection you see in a puddle rather than in a mirror; the type that asks you to stop and stay awhile and consider that this puddle is only there for a short time – the image reflected will eventually dry up and go.

Place is important. Outside the Hall, the name of the Russian socialist writer and thinker Maxim Gorky is painted on the façade. So the romantic idea of writing something from the building's "lower depths" (title of one of Gorky's better-known social-realist plays) always appealed to me. Up the street is the RayCam Co-operative Centre, a very important housing spot and strong community centre. If you go south, you'll hit Strathcona Park, which currently is home to the Indigenous Food Sovereignty Circle. If you walk just a few blocks west, you'll hit Chinatown – an iconic part of Vancouver, now in great danger of being dismantled and gentrified. All of these are located within the area known by the Sḵwx̱wú7mesh People as Khupkhahpay'ay, one of the words in Sḵwx̱wú-7mesh sn̓ichim for "cedar tree" – an apt description for what the landscape used to look like. Sometimes, when I walk through this neighbourhood, I look at the trees and wonder which ones, if any, have been here the whole time.

Place is important. I come back to this. It provides context. It makes things real instead of abstract. It's too easy to get behind an abstract concept. I look at the Russian Hall, the Soviet nostalgia that permeates it, and feel a certain awe and excitement: I've always been a big fan of the idea of communism. Although, later in life, I would meet people who grew up under Soviet occupation – and they didn't give it five stars. But when something is far away and not quite in your reality, it's easier to get behind it. A cause perhaps, a stance, a perspective on society – all very easy to subscribe to when there's distance. But what happens when it's standing right in front of you? Wanting to sit next to you? Do you mind it then? It's easy to say you want a community where the vulnerable are valued, but are you willing to spend time with society's most vulnerable folks? Do you really value them? Or do you only value the idea of them existing? Do you value them also when their opinions don't match yours? Needless to say, I include myself in this path of inquiry.

The image that stays with me the most from *Do you mind if I sit here?* is one of elder abuse. The character of Cosmo, as their name implies, is a cosmonaut, but also the apparent keeper of the place we're in, the place that is being assessed for its potential of what it *could* be. Cosmo carries on their work of maintaining the place as is and thus, in a way, becomes a metaphor for the Russian Hall, as well as a signifier of how things were. When meeting Cosmo, the character of B attempts to get the cosmonaut to leave, first using kindness and patience. But Cosmo does not comply, or even respond, exhibiting a passiveness that increasingly infuriates B. We may admire this image of the past from a distance, but when it contradicts our desires in the present, it becomes an obstacle to be removed.

In this way, what this play performs is a certain hyp-ocrisy, one that I watched being played out quite clearly over the COVID-19 pandemic and thereafter. When given pause, it seemed our collective reaction to the health crisis was a declaration of the better world we wanted, one that rejected capitalism, did away with racism, and called for decolonization. From afar. From within our homes, in iso-lation. But when confronted with the work required to implement such programs – the inconveniences seemed insurmountable.

I don't mean to be so bleak as to imply that there haven't been great steps forward in building empathy and social progress in recent years. But I do mean to say that nostalgia – for the past, of course, but perhaps also for some idea of the future – distracts us from the present. A society where people wouldn't have to experience loneliness and isolation requires a population that will spend time with the lonely and the isolated. Hanging on to just the ideal aspiration gives us an out from taking the actions to achieve it. And so, broadcasting our intent for justice becomes an empty gesture.

At one point, Cosmo, being asked about their isolation by B (whose compassion is by then wavering), extends their arm as if to invite touch – human contact. "I'm sorry, no. We can't do that," says B. "It's to protect all of us." There are limits to compassion, more than we may want to admit. Something I remember vividly from the COVID lockdown was going for walks and actively walking away from people – since that's what it meant at the time to truly be neighbourly. Some of that stayed. You may aspire to a society where everyone lives in dignity, but are you gonna sit next to them on the bus? Place is important – space is important – but for all our aspirations, are we willing to share it?

—Jiv Parasram

DO YOU MIND IF I SIT HERE?

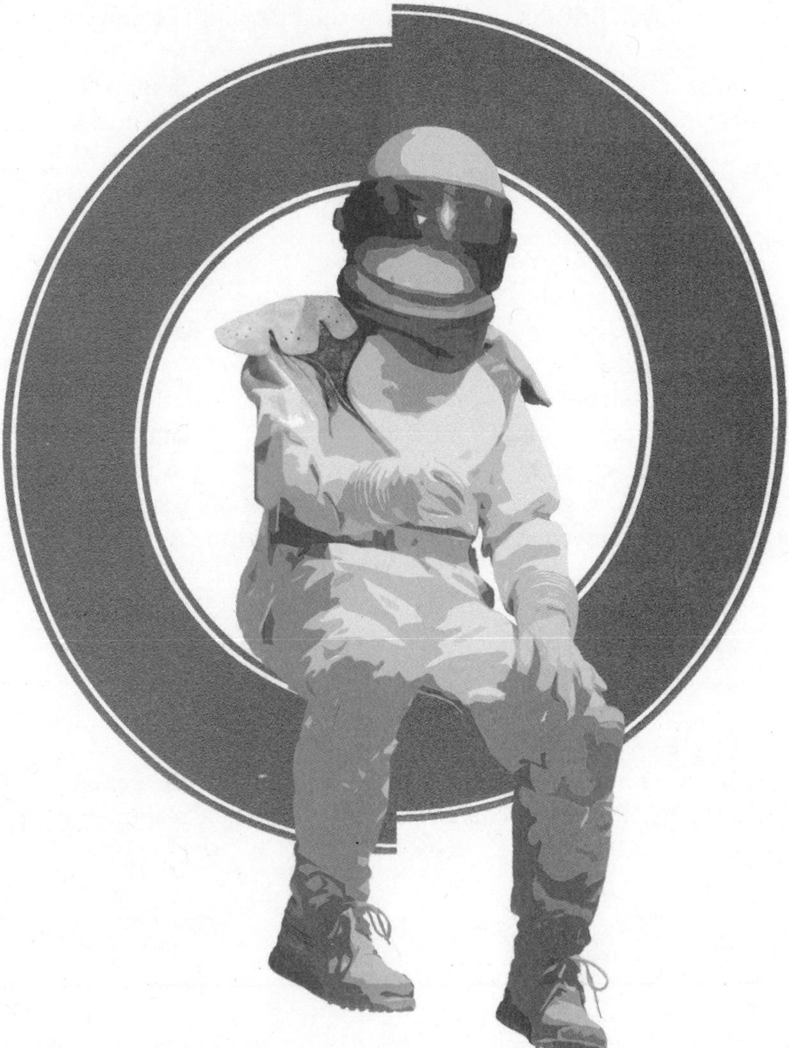

Production History

Do you mind if I sit here? was developed from May 2020 to January 2022 by Theatre Replacement and premiered in January 2022 at the PuSh International Performing Arts Festival in Vancouver, British Columbia, with the following cast and crew:

A	Pippa Mackie
B	Kayvon Khoshkam
C	Conor Wylie
COSMO	Gina Stockdale

Director and Co-Writer	James Long
Co-Writer	Marcus Youssef
Assistant Director	Arthi Chandra
Stage Manager	Melissa McCowell
Video Designer	Candelario Andrade
Sound Designer and Composer	Mauricio Pauly
Lighting Designer	Sophie Tang
Costume Designers	Barbara Clayden and Alaia Harmer
Choreographer	Justine A. Chambers
Technical Director	Matt Oviatt
Audio Engineer	Brad Danyluk
Production Assistant	Jordyn Wood
Producer	Corbin Murdoch

Do you mind if I sit here? was developed with the generous support of the National Arts Centre's National Creation Fund.

Characters

A, a social planner
B, a social planner
C, a social planner and "Presencer," younger than the others
COSMO, an elderly cosmonaut
OTHER COSMO is played by **A**. This is only revealed to
  the audience when **A** removes their helmet.
FREE indicates that any of **A**, **B**, or **C** can speak the line.

Setting

The Russian Hall (also known by some as the Russian People's home), a cultural centre in Vancouver, British Columbia, long abandoned due to damage from earthquakes and flooding.

This play takes place in the year 2052 ... or so.

Production Design

All of the projections indicated in the script are from 16 mm films from the USSR that were found by the writers in a closet of the Russian Hall.

Production Notes

On Overlapping Dialogue
A double foreword slash, //, is used in this text to indicate a point where one character's dialogue overlaps another's.

On Pronouns
As a nod to the future, we have chosen to use the gender-neutral singular personal pronouns *they*, *them*, and *themself* throughout the text, with the exception of words spoken by **COSMO**.

INTRODUCTION

The audience enters the space.

*Tables are set up in a large square on the
perimeter of the space with seating for as many
as can fit, up to a hundred. It is a show for a
smaller audience.*

*At each seat is a bowl, a shot glass, and a spoon,
along with a small pencil and four Post-it notes.
Hanging in the centre of the room is a cluster
of speakers allowing for loud and exceptional
sound. On the two longer sides of the space,
there are projection surfaces ten feet high that
run the length of the tables. On the ends, the
screens are smaller and have a more typical 4:3
aspect ratio.*

*The long screens are filled with slow-moving
images of clouds.*

There are ten chairs in the playing area.

The audience settles. A swell of music.

ACT 1 SCENE ONE

Do you mind if I sit here?

A enters.

*A begins speaking the text. The following,
never identical, is repeated for the entrances
of B and C and builds over the sequence. Each
of the actors wears a highly sensitive lavalier
microphone that allows them to speak in a quiet
and intimate manner.*

A
Sometimes I can be a little bit like this.
Sometimes it can show up like this.
But it's normally more like this.
Or this.
If I'm upset or something, it can go …
But never …
That's not true.
Because I have done this.
Once.
Oh, and this.
But if I was to say something like this …
I'd do this.
Or this.

Yeah.
Because, look at this.

B enters.

A and B see each other.

The text continues and begins to include the occasional insertion of third-person pronouns, interspersed with the first person. Overlapping voices. A, B, and C catch each other's rhythms in movement and speech. They respond to each other on occasion – a fast to a slow, a big to a big. This is a binary.

A and **B**
Sometimes I/they can be a little bit like this.
Sometimes it can show up like this.
But it's normally more like this.
Or this.
If they're upset or something, it can go ...
But never ...
That's not true.
Because I/they have done this.
Once.
Oh, and this.
But if I was to say something like this ...
I'd do this.
Or this.
Yeah.
Because, look at this.

C enters without a chair. A problem. Maybe C forgot? Maybe they were not aware of the rules.

A, B, and **C**
(*voices overlapping*) Sometimes I/they can be a little bit like this.

[8]

Sometimes it can show up like this.
But it's normally more like this.
Or this.
If I'm upset or something, it can go ...
But never.
That's not true.
Because I/they have done this.
Once.
Oh, and this.
But if I was to say something like this ...
I'd do this.
Or this.
Yeah.
Because, look at this.

> *C attempts to sit in the others' chairs. Things escalate until the sound is sucked out of the room.*

SCENE TWO
Welcome to the Hall:
A History, Engagement One

*The space comes alive. Still images of the naked Hall are projected on the long screens. When the speaker is listed as **FREE**, this allows either **A**, **B**, or **C** to speak the line.*

B
So, it's important.

A
And when we say "it's important," we mean it's important to us. As Planners.

B
Planners in charge of your Urban Spaces.
To encourage your investment.

A
This is about you.

B
You,

A
You,

B
Because every plan.

A
Like every building.

B
Or person.

A
And person.
Every plan is a process.
We process. We work with process.

C
Processes.

B
To develop plans with the public. And when we say "public,"
we mean you. All of you.
In buildings.

A
Yes.
Like this.
Like this.

C
Plans. Living plans that can be modified.

B
But ultimately followed.

C
Yes,

A
Yes,
And but,

B
But when we say "process," then we will always say,

A
Welcome.

B
Yes. But,

A
But before,

B
And before.
As part of this welcome,

C
An acknowledgment. Of history.

B
Yes, of Land. Of trees and people and Territories.

A
Territory.
Unceded Territory.
Stolen Land.

B
Yes.

C
Yes.

A
Yes.

B
Some say "acknowledge." Some say "thank you."

A

It shows up like this.

*With each "this" spoken, the actor demonstrates
a subtle gesture or physical shape that sits
somewhere between shame and gratitude.*

C

And like this.

A

And like this.

B

And this.
What we continue to say. To repeat, is:

FREE

The Sḵwx̱wú7mesh and xʷməθkʷəy̓əm and səlilwətaɬ.[1]
The Sḵwx̱wú7mesh and xʷməθkʷəy̓əm and səlilwətaɬ.
The Sḵwx̱wú7mesh and xʷməθkʷəy̓əm and səlilwətaɬ.
The Sḵwx̱wú7mesh and xʷməθkʷəy̓əm and səlilwətaɬ.
Yes?
Yes.
Yes.

A

Here.

This place. This building. Tonight.
This moment. Welcome.
Together.

B

Yes, not alone. No one alone. We are three. You are [*speaking
the approximate number of audience members*].

---

1   The phonetic spellings of Squamish, Musqueam, and Tsleil-Waututh. In the
event this piece is performed elsewhere on Ancestral Indigenous lands, a similar
acknowledgment of the respective Indigenous inhabitants is encouraged.

A

Together.

B

And when we say "together," we mean "sitting." Beside
strangers,

> *A, B, and C list random characteristics of*
> *audience members.*

A

Sharing space. Experience. Air. Even air.

B and **C**
In this building.

C

Sorry.

A

This building that has been empty for so long.

B
Too long.
Abandoned.

A
Dormant.

B

And when we say "building," we mean "potential."

A

Social potential.

B

Human potential. We mean repurposing. We mean
imagining.

C

A new beginning.

A

A new future. With all of you.
A community. Coming together.
When we can.
In this building. Here. These ...

C

Bones.

A

A body.
A home.
A centre.

C

Once a cultural centre. With classes and choirs and meetings.

B

And when we say "culture" – the sign says "Russian," so we
say "Russian."

C

Even though some might say "Slavic."

A

And some just say "socialist."

C

Or "communist."

A

Some said "communist."

B

But we will say "community." We will repeat: "community."

C
And honour it. With breath.

They breathe.

A
Community.
All communities.
Identities.
Histories.

B
Experiences.

A
Coming together.
In this space.

B
Many communities coming together to build a single community. A voice.

A
That is our job.

B
And that is why we've invited you – here.
To witness. To contribute.

A
To engage.

B
To invest.

C
And to toast!
Vodka or water.

Both cold.
A choice.

A *and* **B** *start offering vodka or water shots to audience members.*

C

Something for you as a start. But please wait until we speak the toast.
Our way of saying thank you.
And welcome.
And there will be food.
Yes!
Because food is each community and all communities.

And when we say "food," we mean a special offering to honour the history of this place. Borscht. A wonderful and authentic borscht. The very same borscht from a recipe that was cooked and served in this hall for eighty years.

A recipe shared with us by a woman named Judy. A direct link to the original community who occupied this hall from 1948 to 2021.

When we say "Judy," we also mean Judy's mother.
And we also mean Judy's grandmother. Women who cooked in the tiny kitchen in this basement.
When four or five women would cook for three or four hundred of their community. Borscht, perogies, sausage.
Served in this room, here.

C

But tonight, for now, in this building, we will only mean one bowl of borscht, bread, and one cookie. Each. Because when I say, "We only have borscht and bread and one cookie, each," I also mean … scarcity.

A
Scarcity.

C
Scarcity.

A
This is a scarce time.

B
For all of us.
It is important for us to say it. To be allowed to say it.
Scarcity.

FREE
Scarce.
Scarce.
Scarce.

B
Because of –
the weather.

> *Pause.*

> *A low sound enters the space.*

> *They stop and listen to it before continuing. This
> does not just function as an underscore but also
> as an event and foreshadow of the same sound
> that comes at the end of act one as a much more
> substantial sound event.*

A
And the consequences.

> *Pause.*

C
Still.

Pause.

A
When we say "weather," we mean "predicted, expected."
But not "planned for."
And when we say "weather,"

B
We mean "what happened."

A
To us. This city. This idea.

B
This building. It became an emergency shelter.

C
A food distribution centre.
A squat.

B
An abandonment. For thirty years.
This community, your community, was shattered.
So many. Alone.

A
And when we say "alone," we mean "lonely."
Because a building,
like a person, can be lonely.

B
And loneliness is the one thing we cannot afford to have.
We will not have it.
No one can be alone.
Not when we can be together.

A
At least for now.

B
So,
Welcome to now. At last.
A new beginning.

C
We hope.

A
For all of us.
And when we say "us," what we mean is "opportunity."

B
We mean "progress."

> *A, B, and C raise a shot glass to the moment.*

> *Projections begin on all four screens; A, B, and C are not aware of them.*

FREE
Join us. To progress.

> *A, B, and C toast and encourage the audience to shout back.*

AUDIENCE
To progress.

B
A return.
A return to a future of a future we could have never imagined.
To progress.

SCENE THREE
Progress Film

A collage of moving images, coupled with sound, demonstrating the beauty and horror of humanity.

It ends in 1970s Soviet space-program imagery.

SCENE FOUR
Cosmo Complication

We hear the sound of breathing. In and out.

*COSMO enters and walks the space. They are
momentarily confused by chairs scattered over
the floor. We hear garble and other fragments of
sound, occasional blips of language or a hybrid
language. The lights are low and cut Cosmo
off in odd patterns. The lights rise and fall,
echoing the breathing patterns. Then we hear
the fragments of words moving along a spectrum
of intelligibility. Garbled, through to clear
passages.*

COSMO
I wake up.
I don't know how long I've been asleep this time. Or if I
should call it sleep. It's not really sleep. It just ... is.
Decades and decades and decades in this ... place. Caring for
this place. This ground. Watching. My home.
I wake up and try to remember the order of the letters *A*, *B*,
C, *D*. *A*, *B*, *C*, and *D*, but then there is the pause.

I wake up.

And try to feel my foot. I could still move my left ... bottom
of the leg. But that could have been a year, or years.
A, B, C ... D.
And last night, last night, last night I heard the words
"superconductor," "Jazzercise," and a prolonged
"haaaaaaaa ..."
And I know they are mine, but I hear so much,
so many and the longer I float ...

SCENE FIVE
A Suit

A, B, and C appear and approach **COSMO.**

A
They're wearing a suit.

B
That's not a suit.

C
Technically, it is a suit.

B
What do they call you again? A presenter?

C
Presencer. I'm here to encourage presence, listen, and respond.

B
You're right. It is a suit. When I said "suit," I meant a different kind of suit.

C
My sense is you were thinking of a business suit.

B
The normal kind of suit.

C
Normal?

B
My apologies. Common. Commonplace.

A
It's an astronaut suit. For going into space.

B
Why an astronaut suit? Any thoughts?

A
Protection.

B
Against what?

A
The heat this summer was crippling.

C
Crippling?

A
I'm sorry. Punishing. The heat would have been awful in here.

C
The heat was very intense.

B
If we could please focus.

A

It could be to protect them from asbestos. You should order a remediation report. I'm sure this building is full of it.

B

We'd have to pause everything, again. For who knows how long.

> *C approaches* **COSMO.**

C

Hello. Can you hear me?

B

(*to* **C**) What are you doing?

> *C raises their hand to stop* **B** *from speaking.*

C

(*to* **COSMO**) I can see and hear you. Can you see or hear me?

A

The suit makes me think of my grandfather. I was with him when he died.

C

Was that why you took a leave?

A

Yes.

B

Two leaves.

A

Three.

C

That's a lot of leaves.

A

I saw him pass into another realm. Ascend into outer space.

C

Did you see his spirit?

A

"Spirit" is not the right word.

C

Thank you for letting me know that. What other word might you use?

A

I'm not sure. Why?

C

It's what's occurring, what came up for you. It could be significant.

B

Getting back to the task at hand – I feel some concern that we're fucked.

A

We might want to reconsider our approach.

B

I don't think that's necessary.

> *COSMO stands up and begins to walk, but after a few steps they sag. A goes to get COSMO a chair.*

B
No. Leave them.

A
Sit.

B
Stop.

A
It's okay.

A has seated **COSMO.**

B
(*to* **A**) I thought you wanted to move forward, get things done.

A
It's our job to include them, learn what they need.

B
What about the community?

A
Aren't they part of the community?

B
I don't see any evidence that they are.

C
You should start with the larger community.

B
Fine.

C
It's your impulse. We'll begin here.

B
Quickly. Please.

A
We'll take whatever time we need.

SCENE SIX
Contact

COSMO
There is a door over there. And four stairs.
A bed frame, wires, broom, a pommel horse. Wires. And
twenty-four cans of film.

> *C readies themself to presence, to listen deeply.*
> *Film clips of what appears to be a hospital for*
> *blind children appear on the small screens.*
> *A observes.*

COSMO
I watch this one because the boy looks happy.
He's blind. Simple.
The doctors ...
... happy ... People should see. Who doesn't want to see? ...
Little boys are happy ... children everywhere ...

... falling in love ...

> *A new film depicting a clown entertaining*
> *children takes over.*

COSMO
Oh, and this one, more children. Healthy. A show I used to
watch ... trying to teach me French ... many more children.
The children ... children ... children ... good behaviour ...

> *A new film depicting a northern Indigenous population.*

COSMO
The costumes. Intricate, so beautiful ... dancing ... how they lived. Noble. So dignified.

> *A new film depicting a couple walking through a field and then a deep well.*

COSMO
This one is just a story. It hasn't broken ... love story ... in nature ... getting married and ... and carrying on ... Simple ... Simple. I like the ... well. How deep it is. How long it takes for the bucket to come up. And the reflection of the light on the water.

> *The film runs.*

COSMO
All the fear.

> *Continues running.*

COSMO
Completely fallen apart.

> *COSMO exits. B returns to the room.*

B
What's your assessment? Are they part of the larger community?

C
Their thoughts are disjointed. They don't seem to listen, or even hear.

A

They're old.

C

They're nostalgic for a world that // was built on other people's suffering.

A

It's their memories. The world they grew up in. What they knew.

C

And what comes up for me is a curiosity. And when I say "curiosity," what I mean is a position. How much effort should we be putting into preserving this connection?

A

What do you mean?

C

The world they grew up in is what's destroying our world.

A

That's not their fault.

C

They're clearly isolated here. Holed up. Alone. The language is problematic.

A

They're old. Old people get isolated.

C

I know they do.

A

How many old people do you know? Spend time with on a regular basis?

C

It might be helpful to have some input from you, to get your perspective.

B

We have an engagement to deliver – to the larger community. We need to start.

C

I hear that. I agree. I think we do.

B

And you?

A

We should continue.

SCENE SEVEN
A Toast

Lights back up on the audience.

B
To you.
Each and every one of you.
And this place ...
which is yours.
Which you will help us make in your image.
According to your wishes.
And your needs.
A place for all of us.
To be together.
Not alone.
Never alone.
When we have one another, we will never be alone.

C
Okay, let's eat.

B
We can't. We can't do the soup, real food.

C
We can.

B

No. To eat the soup they'd have to remove their masks. They remove their masks, they breathe. They breathe, we're liable. I'm sorry, but we can't do your soup.

C

But the notice we circulated promised soup.

B

It did. And things changed.

C

It's a good soup.

B

I think everyone understands why we can't serve the soup.

C

I don't know if that's true. I'm sensing that it's just you who does not want me to serve the soup. My soup.

B

Hey.

C

I'm just asking for a little space. I think there could be a really interesting conversation here.

B

Okay, but there will be no soup. I can't do anything about the soup.

C

This is a choice.

B

It's a rule.

C

If we were to ask the people present whether they would be willing to try the soup, I bet more than half would be willing to eat the soup.

B

We won't be doing that.

C

It would be useful data. How the majority really feels. Can we just try?

A

Talk about the soup.

C

But when we say "soup," what comes up is "eating." "Tasting." "Sharing."

B

You are aligning with them on the soup?

A

I'm just asking them to tell us about the soup. Just tell us about your soup.

C

I'm sorry but this is just –

A

Describe the soup.

C

It's soup. You're supposed to eat it.
With your mouth.
It's basic. And when I say "basic," what I mean is "resistance." I mean "justice."

A

Borscht is a soup of the imagination.

C

Sure. but it doesn't work unless // you eat it.

A

Look at us.
We can't even see their faces.
I can't see if they're smiling or bored.
How old they are.
If they have a moustache or lipstick.
Are they listening?

A

We have to imagine. And if there has ever been a time for
the imagination, it is right now. And the power of collective
imagination.

Imagine the cart. Your cart over there.
Imagine pushing that cart.
And holding a ladle.
And dipping that ladle into the pot and pulling up your
remarkable borscht.

A switches their focus towards the audience.

Imagine that borscht filling that bowl in front of you. Right
to the edge.
It's warm. It's rich.
Cooked in an old way. From a recipe a woman named Judy
inherited from her grandmothers.

Imagine this hall a hundred years ago. Full. Four hundred
people. Russians, Belarussians, Ukrainians, and people from
the neighbourhood.

It's their borscht. Remembering what this building once
was will help us decide what we want it to become. Not
alone. Together.
Okay?

C
Okay.

A
The primary value is community.

> *A film begins. It is an English-language
> documentary showing the success of Soviet
> communal living. The film includes street scenes,
> scenes from schools, a marriage, and children's
> camps. The original voice-over (**VO**) plays.*

VO
Let's get acquainted.
We all live on the same planet. Perhaps our climate, customs,
and outlooks are different, but we all have the same cares
and worries.
We both grieve misfortune and rejoice in success.
We all tend to love and quarrel alike.
In what way do we differ, then?
There are over two hundred and thirty million of us Soviet
people today.
So let's get acquainted.

We all look alike. Unfortunately, not only the children, but
the homes too.
Such is reality.
Four point five million children are born in our country
annually, and they all need a home.

When two people fall in love, life in a tent seems
like paradise.

But the moment they marry, they demand a two-bedroom
apartment with all conveniences.

Our housing problem is not as acute as before.
And now we can give more attention to beautifying our
streets and towns …

It is hard to say who was the first to begin this, adults
or children.
However, the youngsters aren't interested in priorities.
We learn independence from a very early age, and value it
above all else.
Let us hope she will grow up to be a good homemaker.

SCENE EIGHT
Abatement

*At a certain point during the showing of the films, **COSMO** enters and begins to clear up the bowls in a clumsy fashion. **A**, **B**, and **C** watch **COSMO**. The sound from the film fades to a murmur.*

B

I think we need to consider removal.

C

Do we have that authority?

B

We do if they are an impediment to the repurposing.

A

My sense is they are part of this community.

B

Watch how they move. What they notice, attend to. Or not. Are they receiving information from others? Are they capable of dialogue? Authentic exchange?

A

They speak. They have language.

C

Can we find them a home? A nice room. With a microwave, and a sink. A bed. The company of others like them.

B

That could take months.

A

Years. Power of attorney, waiting lists.

B

They would remain on our file. Our responsibility. Indefinitely.

C

I didn't realize.

A

I wanted to put my grandfather in a home. A nice room. With a microwave, and a sink. A bed. The company of others like them.

B

Did you find him a place?

A

I tried for years. A nice room. With a microwave, and a –

C

What I am hearing is that it was a difficult process.

A

It was.

B

You took a leave.

C
Two leaves.

A
Three.

C
Three leaves. That's a lot of leaves.

A
I made a decision.

C
About your grandfather?

A
Yes.

B
Because he was lonely.

A
It went on for a very long time.

B
You acted.

A
Yes.

B
You made a designation.

A
I did.

B
Of acute loneliness.

A

Abject. The correct designation is: abject.

B

Abject.

> *Beat.* **A** *nods.*
>
> *The weather-rumble sound heard near the end
> of scene two returns. It slowly rises in volume
> and continues into the next scene.*

B

These decisions are not easy.

A

He was suffering.

B

Do they seem similar in some ways? Your grandfather, and
this person in a suit? Please be honest.

C

It's important that we are transparent with each other.
Vulnerable, even.

> **B** *notes the growing sound.*

B

Should we pause to let this pass?

A

No.

A

Our values have to include care and compassion.

B

Of course, and it is with care and compassion that I am
speaking. It could also be cruel to prolong this person's
condition. And we have a responsibility to make an
assessment. It's very simple. Five or six questions. I can pull
up the form.

A

Have you ever assisted in another person's death?

> *B doesn't answer. They probably haven't.*
> *A focuses on C.*

A

Have you? It changes you. Or, I should say, it changed me.

C

You watched your grandfather's not-spirit ascend into
outer space.

A

I never said "not-spirit." That's not a word I would use.

C

I was trying to find a non-word that reflected what
you meant.

> *A shakes their head.*

A

I would like to recuse myself from this process.

B

You can't. All three of us have to participate in this decision
for it to hold.

A

I don't feel equipped.

B

You are the most equipped.

C

What I'm hearing is, "let's take a breath."

B

I am breathing.

C

A pause.

B

What about the community?

C

They can wait.

B

The community is always being asked to wait.

C

A brief pause.

A

A real community includes the needs of everyone, even the most vulnerable. Especially the most vulnerable.

B

Is this about your grandfather? Because it's –

C

A pause. Please.

> *They pause and the sound builds, but they ignore it.*

B

Do you agree that a designation of abject loneliness is possible for this individual? Based simply on what we have observed?

A

Yes.

B

I can assess their loneliness. Whether or not it qualifies as abject.

A

Without bias.

B

Without bias. Then we can reconvene and consider how best to move forward.

C

Together.

B

Yes. We need this to be together.

SCENE NINE
A Deep Rumble

The deep rumble in the building continues and builds.

It is obvious that this is not the first time this noise has happened.

C
Excuse me.

C moves to the centre of the room and starts to hum.

B
(*listening*) They're doing that young person thing. They say it's not prayer. But it is.

A
I read that they are now connecting these weather events directly to soil temperature.

B
And the core. Core and soil.

A
And also the ocean. I've heard it is connected to the ocean.

A starts moving towards C. C notes that A has joined them.

C

"Holy." I say "holy."

A

"Holy"?

C

It's the word I use to try to understand these things.

A

"Holy."

C

And when I say "holy," I mean –

A

"Holy."

C

Yeah. It's the right word.

The sound continues to grow. A series of images come up on the screens. It grows and grows into a monumental collage of apocalyptic film clips. A and C exit halfway through. The volume increases to an almost unbearable level and the images culminate in a herd of buffalo circling the space.

ACT2 SCENE ONE
Engagement Three

B

(*to the audience*) Sorry for how long this is taking.
There are always a lot of moving parts in a project like this.
Particularly one of this scale. And when I say "scale," I mean
"complexity." And when I say "complexity," I mean "weight,"
I mean "status."
I mean "real."

What you are not seeing here are the twelve years of
assessments.
Of trying to track down ownership of this building. Finding
out there was no real ownership.
Of reassessments under new guidelines and ... it's not easy.
It shouldn't be.

But if there is anything I have learned in my many – and its
many – years in this work, is that there is always an outcome.
There is.
Something always happens.

In front of each of you are sanitized pencils and Post-it notes.
A bit old-school, maybe. I still like the tactile.

I need you to help us envision a new future for this building.
One that is free of limitations.
I want you to write them down.

What can this building be? A daycare? A library?
Write it down.
And when I say "a daycare" or "a library," what I mean is "a
café" and "a bouncy castle."

COSMO *enters.*

B
I mean "a time machine" and "a green roof." "An employment
centre" and "a squash court." What I mean is "a tool library"
and "a friendship centre" and "a mosque" …

What do you love? Just write it down.
What do you like?
What do you need?

What you want is what this building needs. What we all need.
Even if we don't know it yet.

When you are done – just put them on the table in front of
you so we can come by, pick them up, and try and imagine
how this might happen for you. For this community.

Remember: your visions of the future will tell us how to
behave, right now, in the present.

SCENE TWO
Cosmo as Encounter

COSMO begins to move chairs.

B
Don't do that. Please.
I'm going to sit here, okay?

COSMO keeps working on the chairs.

B
I need to ask you a few questions.
And, um, before we start, I want to say thank you for all the
work you continue to do on behalf of this building. It is noted
and appreciated.

COSMO drags a chair, loudly.

B
It is a remarkable space and I'm sure it wouldn't still be so
without your efforts.

*B tries to get their attention, but COSMO keeps
moving.*

B
I need you to stop moving, please.

COSMO *pivots away.*

B
Oh, for fuck's sake.

COSMO *continues to move.*

B
Please sit.

> *After an extended period of wandering,*
> **COSMO** *sits on a chair in the corner of the*
> *playing space.* **B** *also sits.*

B
Let me start by saying this building, and when I say
"building," I mean *building* – roof, floor, walls – is a very
important building. A building that has been scheduled for
some time now to benefit a returning community.

> **COSMO** *stands and moves towards* **B** *on the*
> *chair.* **B** *eventually stands.*

B
And when I say "community," I mean "a community
comprised of various individual communities with differing
priorities making up a single community."

> **COSMO** *moves* **B**'s *chair.*

B
You can't stay here. Not like this.
I think you know that.

> **COSMO** *registers this in some way but doesn't*
> *respond.*

> **B** *gets* **COSMO** *a chair.*

B
Now let me get you a chair.
Please sit.

>   *COSMO walks to B and the new chair.*

B
Sit!

>   *COSMO sits.*

B
Do you have somewhere that you could go? A relative or a
friend we could try and contact for you?

>   *B moves their own chair closer to the centre of
>   the stage and sits across from COSMO.*

B
I'm going to ask you some questions. To assess how you are
doing. The extent of what appears to be a significant state of
loneliness.
You know what that means? "Loneliness"?

It would be so helpful for me if you could remove
your helmet.

>   *COSMO takes a long moment before slightly
>   pivoting their head.*

B
All right.

Question one: Do you live with anyone? Is there anyone else
living in this building with you?

>   *No answer.*

B

Okay, two: Do you have anyone you talk to who does not live with you?

Someone who you run into and know well enough to speak to?

> **COSMO** *still says nothing.*

B

Question three: How often do you attend gatherings? They can be of any kind.
Religious services?
Clubs?
Miscellaneous organizations?
Four: When was the last time you went outside?

Out there.

> *B stands up and points to the door.* **COSMO**
> *twists a bit to their left.*

B

Do you ever go out there?

Do you ever see other people?
See them seeing you?
See them looking at what you wear. Do you ever imagine what their life is like, how it might be different than yours, or maybe almost exactly the same?

> **COSMO** *sits up and looks at* **B.**

B

When did people stop visiting you?

> *No answer.*

Images of dancing women come up onscreen.
COSMO stands and holds out their arm. B is
not interested in contact.

B
I'm sorry, no. We can't do that.

COSMO tries again.

B
It's to protect all of us.

Beat.

Thank you.

B exits and COSMO begins a movement
sequence. It's slow and careful, more of a
shaping of space than any kind of recognizable
dance. Over time it begins to echo the muted,
black-and-white films that come up on the
longer screens showing women learning
traditional Slavic dances. These films loop and
abstract.

SCENE THREE
Radical Empathy

A second, identical **COSMO** *enters the space.*

COSMO *sees* **OTHER COSMO** *enter the middle of the room. They face and move around each other. Light and sound allow the two to be mistaken for one another. Both look old. Both look young. They move faster, beyond a speed that an older* **COSMO** *should move.*

One stops the other with a touch.

The touch causes the other to melt.

We are not sure which one is which.

One lies down.

B *and* **C** *enter.*

SCENE FOUR
A Meal

*We hear **A**'s voice.*

A
There must be a small room, somewhere. A small room with a microwave, and a bed? The company of others like them.

B
I don't see it happening.

A
I felt them. Beneath the suit. It felt like, what I might call, a … ?

C
Pulse. That's the word you mean. A pulse.

A
No, that's not what I meant. It was hard to tell at first. And it felt …

C
Yes?

A
Holy. It felt holy.

C

A pulse can be holy. It can be overwhelming even.

A

And it was consistent. What I felt.

C

Would you call it "undeniable"?

A

Do you mean "present"? Because it was there. And it was consistent.

C

When I say "undeniable," what I mean is "essential."

A

I didn't have a lot of time with them. And they're old.

C

They are. Very old. Did it feel essential?

> The **COSMO** on the ground sits up and removes
> their helmet. It is **A**.

C

Did you feel like you needed it?

A

Needed?

C

To feel better. Did you need them to feel better?

A

It wasn't about me.

C

You want to connect. I know that feeling. Particularly when you share qualities with someone. A commonality.

A

"Commonality"?

C

What happened with your grandfather.

A

That's not what I was doing.

C

But it is what I am seeing. A struggle. And it's important to recognize when it's not actually there. That this need to always be in a positive relationship to others, no matter who they are … it doesn't work. You have to draw a line when the people you are trying to connect with begin hurting you. Hurting the larger community.

A

But they're just old.

C

Yes, and very, very alone. Abjectly alone.

B

So, are we okay to start?

C

I feel comfortable in saying yes.

A

I want to see the assessment.

B

It's in the file.

A

Did they understand what was happening?

B

Absolutely. This is the best decision for everyone.

A

What is?

> *B pauses.*

B

Helping them.

> *B and C each pick up a chair.*

A

Say it.

B

Assisting. We're assisting.

A

The larger community?

B

No, them. Yes. And the community. Yes. And. Always. Both.

> *B and C place the chairs facing each other as though two people might sit for an intimate conversation.*

A

Just say what you are doing. Speak it.

B

We are moving forward.

A turns to C.

A
Is this what you're hearing?

C
It's what's happening.

A
I don't support it.

B
That's why there are three of us.

>*C invites **COSMO** to sit in one of the two chairs.*

C
Hi there. Do you want to come over here? Sit down?
That's right.
You work so hard.

>*COSMO moves towards the two chairs, then subtly adjusts their trajectory to follow **B** and **C** as the two begin leaving the room. As the three exit, **B** and **C** continue speaking as though they were seating and feeding **COSMO** in the empty chairs they just set up. **A** also responds to the action as if it were happening in those empty chairs. A dislocation of space.*

B
No, this one.
You want to sit in this one.

C
Just sit down.

B
Okay, we're going to have to take this helmet off.
No, it's okay.

C
Just relax.

B
We brought this for you. Some soup.

C
It's warm.

After a certain age, two, maybe three years old, we don't get to enjoy this, do we? Here you go.

A
They're spilling.

C
It's okay.

A
They're spilling it!

C
Shh …

> **A** *begins removing the Cosmo suit they were*
> *wearing and moves to sit in a chair at the edge*
> *of the space.* **C** *returns to the room and collects*
> *the Post-it notes.*

SCENE FIVE
Community

Lights. **C** *hands the stack of Post-it notes to* **B**, *who has re-entered.* **B** *reads a few as he walks the space.*

B

Wow. I've completed so many of these processes, and when I say "processes," I also mean "processes," the many plurals of "process," and I never stop looking forward to reading what people suggest.

(*reading one of the Post-it notes*) "A building where *everyone* is welcome."

And whoever wrote that underlined "everyone." And those reminders of the community context are so important. So, thank you for that.

> **B** *hands a pile to* **C**, *keeping the rest for themself.*

B
(*to* **C**) Go ahead.

> *The following are examples of suggestions as written by the audience during the initial run of the show.*

C
"A daycare centre."

B
"An artspace."

C
"A meeting place."

B
"A shelter."

> *B goes to A and hands them a pile. A takes it.*
> *B waits, but A doesn't say anything.*

B
"A hospital."

C
"Lots of stuff around that you can just use without asking permission."

B
"A Kitten Café."

C
"A gym."

B
"A prayer room."

C
"Lots of bright colours; kids' art on the walls."

B
"An accessible space."

C
"Housing for single mothers."

B
"An escape from extreme heat."

C
"A hospice."

> **B** *stops and looks at* **A**, *waiting for them to contribute.*

A
"A preschool."

C
Thank you.

B
"A tower."

C
"A restaurant that sells food at cost."

B
"A library."

C
"Housing for the DTES."[2]

B
"A quiet space."

---

2   Downtown Eastside, by many accounts Vancouver's poorest and most complex neighbourhood.

C

"Anti-capitalist."

A

"A food bank."

C

"An anarchist space."

B

"Meditation space."

C

"Air conditioning. And better heat!"

A

"A green roof."

C

"Don't waste time with long boring meetings."

B

"Open-minded."

C

"Somewhere to rest."

> *From back behind the stage, some banging and clanging begins. It gets closer as the list continues. A stops contributing and moves towards the sound. B and C soldier on.*

B

"Toilet-seat warmers."

C

"A safe space."

B

"Collective."

C

"Anti-racist."

B

"A supervised injection site."

C

"Carbon-neutral."

B

"A maker lab."

C

"Housing for refugees."

B

"One of those places you can scream and pound pillows with no one hearing."

C

"An employment centre."

B

"Not top-down."

C

"*Very* green."

B

"Somewhere to dream big."

C

"A big garden."

B

"A cat library."

C

"Place to develop skills."

> *The banging increases.* **A** *starts towards the door.*

C

"Three interlocking bunkers with secret passcodes."

B

"Climate control."

C

"A sensory deprivation tank."

B

"Free meals twenty-four hours a day. Nutritious ones. But also tasty!"

B

"Somewhere to gather and meet new people."

C

"Cozy."

B

"A something (*having trouble deciphering*) university." "A Free University"!

C

"A yoga studio."

> **COSMO** *emerges from the doorway dragging a large blanket filled with random objects.*
>
> *It's pretty operatic.*

B

"Mad-friendly."[3]

C

"Warm."

B

"Zero tolerance for hate."

C

"Its own currency but not digital."

B

"Warmth, comfort."

C

"A place to connect."
(*aside, to* **B**) These ideas are terrific.

> *A responds to* **COSMO** *coming across the floor.*
> *They are unsteady but moves towards them.*

B

(*to* **C**) Yes. So many.

C

So much to process. *Processizing.* Consciously. Somatically.
With your friends.

B

Yes.

C

Yes.

---

3   "Mad" is used as a Mad Pride–aligned reclamation of the term for those
historically labelled as mentally "ill".

B

With your friends.

> *B enters into a conversation with **A**. **C** continues
> with the audience. **COSMO** begins making their
> way to the ground. **A** will lie down with them.*

B

They were lying down when I left the room.

A

You needed to lie down beside them.

C

We will provide all the necessary channels for your continued
engagement.

A

It helps them to stay calm.

C

If you go to our website, you'll find a short survey.

B

I didn't know.

C

It will take no more than ten minutes of your time.

A

This is it. Their soul is about to ascend into outer space.

> *A holds **COSMO** as they relax into stillness.*

C

Beautiful. A lot to process, contend with. And beautiful.
Thank you.

B
Yes. Thank you.

C
Just before we wrap up. Do you mind?

    B nods. They're done.

SCENE SIX
Cookies

C
Would you mind getting the cookies? Handing them out?
It's fine, they're individually wrapped.

> *B gets individually wrapped chocolate-chip
> cookies and starts handing them out to the
> audience members. A stays with **COSMO**.*

A
(*to C*) We need to call someone.

C
Absolutely. Just give me a second. I got this.
(*to the audience*) Our final offering. One you can eat.
You can take it home. If you choose.

I made them. Last night, when I was preparing the borscht
and I want to honour that. For a minute. If that's all right. (*to
A*) To imagine?

Shall we take a breath? Together? If you choose.

These cookies are my mom's recipe.
Flour, butter, sugar, chocolate chips. Designed and created.
By me. According to a design passed down to me.

C watches B hand them out.

C

Take a look across the room. At anyone. Look at them. You don't have to make eye contact. But take a breath and just look at them. Think about them. Their hair. Their hands. How blood moves through their veins. How the nerves in their bodies are telling them they are sitting on a chair. In a room. In a building that no one has sat in for so, so long. Too long.

Look right at that person's eye.

An eye. An eye. How it grew in a womb, was assigned a colour, a shape. How it learned to open and close, to see. Or not see. How it communicates back to the brain with electrical currents. How the brain then applies language, language shaped by the language of its ancestors, its family, whatever that may have been – in order to make sense of the information it is trying to process.

That chain of information, from light to energy to language is infinitely more complex than the cookie you have in front of you. That cookie that I made. Designed and made.

Isn't it also possible some *thing* made that eye as well? Or allowed for its design? Some *thing* we will never fully understand but is ultimately responsible for all of us and all that we do?

Something holy.
A reassurance.
That all these individual choices we believe we are making – this cookie or that cookie, this building, that building – all these little rights and wrongs, are not truly in our control after all.

They're not. That's what I believe. We are part of something bigger than that. We are ...

And that thing. That holy, glorious thing is community.
That is the only thing that makes us remarkable.

Or do we prefer the alternative?

That we are just a series of individual needs.
Individually responsible for each and every single one of our
own actions and that's it?

No.
No.
No.
No one ever has to be that alone.

THE END

FEDERATION OF RUSSIAN CANADIANS
JULY 22, 1945

ORCHESTRA
FEDERATION OF RUSSIAN CANADIANS
VANCOUVER B.C. MARCH 1950

RUSSIAN-LANGUAGE SCHOOL, 1960-61,
TEACHER JOHN SHARKO.
VANCOUVER, B.C.

Acknowledgments

First and foremost, we would like to thank the Russian Hall and its many, many volunteers who have lovingly cared for the space for close to eighty years. As it continues to transition from a culturally specific gathering place for families of various Slavic descent living in the area to an arts and culture centre supporting a vast variety of creative, political, and community acts, the Hall has become essential to Vancouver's creative identity. You really can feel the structure's *soul* every time you enter the building, and it is the true protagonist of this work. As part of that thanks, we would specifically add Craig Boyco, the present live-in caretaker of the Russian Hall, and also the Hall's board of directors for giving us the permission to use its collection of films.

Further thanks to the many artists who contributed to the exploration and development of the work including Carmen Aguirre, Anton Lipovetsky, Omari Newton, and Tia Taurere-Clearsky, and also the many community members who gave feedback on early iterations of the work.

A special thanks also goes to Bard on the Beach, who lent us their remarkable sound system, and Elia Kirby and Great Northern Way for its work on the screens.

A final thanks always goes to our families: Nicky, Nora, and Leo Pontin for continuing to allow me (James) the time and space to follow these creative impulses; and Amanda Fritzlan and Zak and Oscar Youssef for helping anchor me (Marcus) to this place for more than thirty years.

LEFT: Archival images currently displayed in the lobby of the Russian Hall.

JAMES LONG is a director, actor, writer, and teacher whose creative practice occurs in a variety of interdisciplinary and collaborative contexts, including as a founder and now artistic associate of Theatre Replacement and as an independent artist working in live performance, community-engaged practice, and public art. James's work has been presented across North America, Europe, and Asia and includes *Weetube, Footnote Number 12, Clark and I Somewhere in Connecticut, Town Criers, BioBoxes: Artifacting Human Experience, King Arthur's Knight, Morko, Winners and Losers* (published by Talonbooks in 2015), and others. In 2019, he and Theatre Replacement co-artistic director Maiko Yamamoto were awarded the Siminovitch Prize for their work at Theatre Replacement and as freelance artists. Long graduated from Simon Fraser University's Theatre Program in 2000, he received a master's in Urban Studies in 2018 and is currently an Assistant Professor of Theatre and Performance at SFU's School for the Contemporary Arts.

MARCUS YOUSSEF is a writer, actor, and educator whose fifteen or so plays almost always investigate some aspect of otherness or difference. They have been produced in multiple languages in twenty countries across North America, Europe, and Asia, from Seattle to New York to Reykjavik, London, Venice, Hong Kong, Vienna, Athens, Frankfurt, and Berlin. Marcus is the recipient of Canada's most prestigious theatre award, the Siminovitch Prize for Theatre, for his body of work as a playwright, as well as Berlin's Ikarus Prize, the Vancouver Mayor's Arts Award, the Rio Tinto Alcan Performing Arts Award, the Chalmers' Canadian Play Award, the Seattle Times Footlight Award, the Vancouver Critics' Innovation Award (three times), and the Canada Council's Victor Martyn Lynch-Staunton Award. Youssef was artistic director of Neworld Theatre in Vancouver from 2005 to 2019 and co-founded the East Vancouver artist-run production hub Progress Lab 1422. He teaches regularly at the National Theatre School of Canada, UBC, and Studio 58.